RAJ'S RULE

(For the Bathroom at School)

By Lana Button

Illustrated by Hatem Aly

Owlkids Books

To Tod, a funny one for you! — L.B.
For Baba, who cheers me up without fail — H.A.

Text © 2020 Lana Button
Illustrations © 2020 Hatem Aly

Owlkids Books acknowledges the financial support of the Canada Council for the Arts, the Ontario Arts Council, the Government of Canada through the Canada Book Fund (CBF) and the Government of Ontario through the Ontario Creates Book Initiative for our publishing activities.

Published in Canada by
Owlkids Books Inc.
1 Eglinton Avenue East
Toronto, ON M4P 3A1

Published in the United States by
Owlkids Books Inc.
1700 Fourth Street
Berkeley, CA 94710

Library of Congress Control Number: 2019955817

Library and Archives Canada Cataloguing in Publication

Title: Raj's rule (for the bathroom at school) / Lana Button ; illustrated by Hatem Aly.
Names: Button, Lana, 1968- author. | Aly, Hatem, illustrator.
Identifiers: Canadiana 20190239123 | ISBN 9781771473408 (hardcover)
Classification: LCC PS8603.U87 R35 2020 | DDC jC813/.6—dc23

Edited by Debbie Rogosin
Designed by Danielle Arbour

Manufactured in Guangdong Province, Dongguan City, China, in February 2020, by Toppan Leefung Packaging & Printing (Dongguan) Co., Ltd. Job # BAYDC78

A   B   C   D   E   F   G

Publisher of Chirp, Chickadee and OWL | Owlkids Books is a division of bayard canada
www.owlkidsbooks.com

Keep your head down, with your knees in a knot, and sit like a statue that's stuck in one spot.

I feel different.

But now I don't know
what my day will be like
when I don't need to go.

I don't have to rush when I wash, I can linger and soak for a second and scrub every finger.

And since I survived that unplanned bathroom trip,
I'll test out the fountain with one little sip.

There's no sense in wasting this juice and this straw. I might find it tasty.

GULP, GULP, GULP, GULP, AHHHHH.

I kinda can cartwheel!
My friends help me try!

This seat's pretty comfy. This work's sort of fun.

I don't usually finish, but now I'm all done!

School's over already? That's it for today?
I'm not in a burst to get home!

If Mom doesn't mind, I'll stay for a while,
to work on my cartwheel—
and hang out with Kyle!